EARLY BIRD
STORIES™

You Can, Toucan

Early★Reader

First American edition published in 2023 by Lerner Publishing Group, Inc.

An original concept by Jenny Jinks
Copyright © 2023 Jenny Jinks

Illustrated by Amy Zhing

First published by Maverick Arts Publishing Limited

Maverick
arts publishing

Licensed Edition
You Can, Toucan

Lerner Publications Company
An imprint of Lerner Publishing Group, Inc.
241 First Avenue North
Minneapolis, MN 55401 USA

For reading levels and more information, look up this title at www.lernerbooks.com.

Main body text set in Mikado a. Typeface provided by HVD Fonts.

Library of Congress Cataloging-in-Publication Data

Names: Jinks, Jenny, author. | Zhing, Amy, illustrator.
Title: You can, Toucan / Jenny Jinks ; illustrated by Amy Zhing.
Description: First American edition. | Minneapolis : Lerner Publications, 2023. | Series: Early bird readers. Green (Early bird stories) | "First published by Maverick Arts Publishing Limited"—Page facing title page. | Audience: Ages 5–9. | Audience: Grades K–1. | Summary: "Toucan worries he can't do things. But the other jungle animals help him realize he can! This heartwarming tale helps young children learn to read with carefully leveled text"— Provided by publisher.
Identifiers: LCCN 2021055126 (print) | LCCN 2021055127 (ebook) | ISBN 9781728438481 (lib. bdg.) | ISBN 9781728448367 (pbk.) | ISBN 9781728444635 (eb pdf)
Subjects: LCSH: Readers (Primary) | LCGFT: Readers (Publications)
Classification: LCC PE1119.2 .J568 2023 (print) | LCC PE1119.2 (ebook) | DDC 428.6/2—dc23/eng/20211130

LC record available at https://lccn.loc.gov/2021055126
LC ebook record available at https://lccn.loc.gov/2021055127

Manufactured in the United States of America
1-49671-49591-12/2/2021

EARLY BIRD STORIES

You Can, Toucan

Jenny Jinks   illustrated by
Amy Zhing

Lerner Publications ◆ Minneapolis

It was time for Toucan
to learn to fly.

He stepped out of the nest
and flapped his wings.

"I cannot do it!" Toucan said.

"You can, Toucan," said his mom.

"Try again."

Toucan spread his wings wide.

He flapped and flapped.

Up he went.

"I CAN do it!" he said.

Toucan went to play hide-and-seek with Monkey.

"I CAN do it!" said Toucan.

Next, Toucan went to swim in the river.

He dipped his foot in.

But it was too cold and deep.

"I cannot do it!" Toucan said.

"You can, Toucan," said Fish.

"Try again."

Toucan splashed in the river.

He swam all the way across.

"I CAN do it!" said Toucan.

It was time for the jungle party.

Toucan wanted to join in and dance.

He began to tap his feet.

"I cannot . . ." Toucan began,
but he stopped and said,
"I CAN!"

He swirled and twirled.

BANG! CRASH!

"I can do it!" said Toucan.

"I can dance!"

"No, Toucan, you cannot!"

the others said.

Toucan felt sad.

"But you will be good at dancing soon," they said. "Try again!"

Quiz

1. What did Toucan usually say?
   a) "I might do it!"
   b) "I will not do it!"
   c) "I cannot do it!"

2. What advice did everyone give?
   a) "Give up."
   b) "Try again."
   c) "Try something else."

3. What did Toucan find hard about hide-and-seek?
   a) Monkey was cheating
   b) His feathers were too dark
   c) His beak was too big and bright

4. What did Toucan find hard about the river?
   a) It was too cold and deep
   b) It was too fast
   c) It was too dirty

5. What did Toucan do at the party?
   a) Sing
   b) Dance
   c) Play hide-and-seek

EARLY BIRD STORIES™

Leveled for Guided Reading

Early Bird Stories have been edited and leveled by leading educational consultants to correspond with guided reading levels. The levels are assigned by taking into account the content, language style, layout, and phonics used in each book. Visit www.lernerbooks.com for more Early Bird Readers titles!

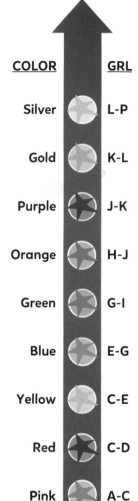

COLOR	GRL
Silver	L-P
Gold	K-L
Purple	J-K
Orange	H-J
Green	G-I
Blue	E-G
Yellow	C-E
Red	C-D
Pink	A-C

Can Dad Dance?

Clumpety Bump

Hoof on the Roof

Snarky Sharky

Whoosh!

You Can, Toucan